Thoughts FROM THE OUTER EDGE OF MY MIND

Thoughts FROM THE OUTER EDGE OF MY MIND

VEESEM

LitPrime Solutions
East Brunswick Office Evolution
1 Tower Center Boulevard, Ste 1510
East Brunswick, NJ 08816
www.litprime.com
Phone: 1-800-981-9893

Published by LitPrime Solutions: 09/27/2024

ISBN: 979-8-88703-402-7(sc)
ISBN: 979-8-88703-403-4(e)

Library of Congress Control Number: 2024917447

Contents

To

Reena, Swaroop and the tiny kids Aadi & Angshu

You Guys, you are so far, yet so
near through your capacity

To Love which is the great inspiration

Acknowledgements

I thank all my lady colleagues Akhila, Raiata,Madhavi, Anitha Milton and Ramya of M/s SFPL for their support and encouragement through patient hearing of my narrations and reading my writings with interest.

My sincere thanks to Mr.Shivu whose encouraging words and guidance helped me to develop the story "Maya The Mohini" in a more meaningful way giving completeness. My special thanks to Latha, my cute and young colleague who is more a mischievous friend than a colleague, without her initiative, meeting Shivu would not have happened.

I thank my niece Baby (Shoba) who volunteered to translate the story " Maya The Mohini" to Kannada language.

My thanks to Chuppi whose encouragement has kept my writing habit alive.

MAYA
THE
MOHINI

I happened to visit my Granny's place sometime back, which is a small town about 300Kms from Bangaluru. A young man visited her house who is a farmer looking after my Granny's lands, one day and wished me. In fact I had seen him a year back in my previous visit. Surprisingly, I could not recognize him immediately due to his entirely changed look. When I had seen him last, he was quite strong, healthy youthful and handsome. In contrast, he was very sick weak and lean this time. I came to understand from Granny that the change in him was due to the entrant of Mohini and he may not survive for long. Also came to know that he had thorough medical check up including a visit to Bangalore and tried various treatments including Ayurvedic and Homeopathy with no positive result. She told me that he is being treated presently by a Tantric.

Mohini as I heard from my Granny is supposed to be the spirit of young lady who had premature death with unfulfilled love in life. It is said that this spirit will be in the form of beautiful woman, always in white dress. Mohini would be wandering in the nights and early mornings in lonely places especially on full moon day looking for young and youthful males. When once this spirit enters a person, he starts loosing interest in life and looses energy gradually turning to sick. If not properly attended well in time it may turn fatal finally.

This interesting information about Mohini from my Granny

inspired me to write this small story. The vital point in this narration being, I have tried to sketch Mohini as a positive energy as against the negative spirit causing harm to the humans, especially the youth, as believed by the people in villages even now.

Maya the Mohini

Our house is situated in a place away from the city. In other words it is in the out skirts of B'lore with more of country side atmosphere than the city surroundings .Hence the prime feature of our area being poor illumination, bad roads, untidy construction etc. There is a big background for constructing this house in this locality. In fact, I had built a descent house in Mysore during the year 1995 with the plan to settle down after retirement, as Mysore is heaven for retired people. .Unfortunately, within an year's time I was called to head office at Bangalore on promotion which I could not deny due to the promotion and also to fulfill the ambition of my wife Sudha to live in Bangalore at least for sometime before we settle down at Mysore. Further, my son got a job in M/s Tata Consultancy Services with a posting at Pune just after completion of engineering at Msore

In the year 1998 after three years working at Bangalore I was expecting transfer back to Mysore. For my shocking surprise I was asked to go to Nagpur. We lived there enjoying extreme weather of Summer and winter. But for the weather Nagpur was a good place to live. During the year 2000, there was a major reshuffle in the Marketing division of the company and in that context I made a request for sending me back to Mysore. For my deep dismay I was called back to Bangalore to head the department with an assured incentive of promotion to Deputy General Manager within six months. Again I missed the chance to return to my home at Mysore.

We were getting used to Bangalore living and also an inclination to settle down at Bangalore was craving in our mind, more so with Sudha. The main reason for this being the chances of Swaroop coming to Bangalore with change of job were brighter than to Mysore. There was a surprising development and Swaroop left to USA for continuation of studies in August 2001.Then, we firmed up our mind to shift the venue for settlement after retirement to Bangalore from Mysore. The house at Mysore fetched a descent returns and hunt for house in Bangalore began. The opinions and difference of opinions thronged between me and Sudha, with me for an apartment and Sudha for an independent house to her taste. Finally, I had to budge to the pressure of a wife and agreed to go for construction of a house within the budget. The problem was getting site and the hunt went on for sometime. With compromise on the location and to suit my pocket we decided on the site where our house stands now. The house was ready with no much hurdles, pretty big for two and we occupied by end of 2002.

As we were in the process of settling down in our new house, there was a major upset in my career and I was asked to go to Singrauli. By that time I was 58 years with only two years left for retirement. There was no other go for me, but to opt for early retirement .After a prolonged resentment and denials I got my Voluntary Retirement and thanks to my Director (Mrktg),but for his strong recommendation it would not have happened.. By end of 2002 my career ended at 58 and was at home as a retired man.

What was destined to happen, happened. Let me come back to my house and its surroundings and then on which is my topic of narration.

After retirement, I was finding a lot of leisure time free of tensions and stresses which made me to look for some activity that takes care of my health and also makes useful occupation of my leisure time. Nevertheless, my wife always kept reminding me of my retirement and attention towards good health. This being the more compelling reason than my own realization which made me to give a serious thought in that direction The simplest of all the exercises at that age I thought was morning walk and was looking for an early start.

My wife left to USA to have some good time with our son, for a long stay of six months. These days I wake up early in the mornings and my repeated attempts to sleep is proving futile. This may be due to loneliness and also the long afternoon sleeps. These early natural wake up calls were the pressing reasons to make up my mind for morning walk.

The sound of alarm made me to wake up suddenly. But it didn't flash to me immediately the reason why the alarm came as a disturbing element in my sound sleep. Quickly I realized it was the D-Day for starting off to my Morning Walk .I woke up from the bed reluctantly and my watch was showing 4.30AM. The cold water of the sink made me to feel fresh to some extent after the wash. I could realize the enjoyment of early morning coffee only after I finished it. It was 5.15AM exact and I stepped out of the house making the eventful beginning.

With lot of search and research I had located a route with the best possible illumination and lesser number of pot holes for my early morning walk of 5Kms.

I was on my maiden morning walk with no humans seen on the way. The occasional barking of dogs and patches of total darkness here and there on the way were scaring at times. Being January, I could see mist also here and there. As my stroll was approaching the end, Dawn's first light spilled giving a delightful look to a portion of the sky. I came back home around 6.15AM covering a distance of about 5Kms.with a satisfaction of a great beginning of an event of my life. The new day was on and I was getting a feeling of brighter days ahead.

The mute mornings and the adorned weather that I always liked, kept my morning walk on without interruptions in spite of minor disturbing incidents now and then. Also, during the walk for more than an hour or so, I would totally be in tranquil mood, due to the quiet moments of the early morning. The serene moments during walk induce me to think about "The remains of the life" with a philosophical approach. Altogether, the habit of morning walk brought a sea change in me. It was unbelievable for my wife Sudha about my habituated morning walk for the past four months, uninterrupted, when she returned from US curtailing her stay from the original plan of six months.

On that day when I came out of the house feeling fresh after my morning coffee, the sky was bright due to Full moon day besides the cool breeze, making the morning totally ideal for a walk .I must have walked about a Km or so, I saw a vague figure coming from the cross road to my right. In a few minutes that figure reached the main road, overtook me and disappeared in the darkness ahead. Though I couldn't see clearly, I made out the person as a young lady in her white track suit. That was the first time I saw somebody coming from that cross road in my morning stroll of more than a year. Then on, I used to see that lady everyday at the junction of that cross road and the main road. It was nearing a month and our meeting at that junction point (which I call as our meeting place) was almost regular; but, none of the two bothered to say 'hello' to each other. In fact, at that wee hour no one used to be seen around, except we two. Also, it was quite surprising to see that lady on jogging alone at that early hour in the area totally dark almost and risky for ladies to move around.

There was too much of barking sound in the surroundings when I stepped out for walk, which was unusual. As I approached the meeting place, I saw that lady coming very much scared, as the dog was chasing her continuously. I whisked away the dog with the batten I had in my hand (I usually carry for my morning walk) and told her to stop for sometime. After a few minutes she just said thanks and continued her jog. I was disappointed at her behavior as I was expecting a formal introduction of ourselves, if not a long talk.

I was feeling uneasy when I got up which was mainly due to the disturbed sleep of previous night. Despite, I decided to go for walk and started late. By the time I reached the meeting place the dawn was just setting in making the morning slightly brighter compared to other days. Surprisingly, I saw that lady also coming at the same time. As she came nearer, she said "Good morning Sir, I am also late today. You know why? I received your telepathy about your late starting. So also I did. Otherwise I would have missed you." smiled and continued without even waiting for my reaction. Her wit was unsavory but her looks were scintillating. The closer look of her which I wanted to have from quite sometime was amazing. She was in her twenties with a perfect physique, bright eyes, inviting lips with a charming complexion More than that her face was radiant and glowing which is unusual. In other words, she was one of the few beautiful ladies I had ever seen. At home when I narrated the incident and about her looks my wife gave a fitting reply "Hello, my dear husband, be careful with that lady, she may fool you one day."

There was a welcome change in her attitude from the day next and she started wishing me regularly "Good morning sir, how are you doing this morning" and also say "Bye" before over taking me. I just used to reciprocate by wishing "Good morning".

When I reached the meeting place I saw that lady standing. She wished 'Good morning' and said "How come you are late? It looks you want to talk to me?"

I was perplexed and said "No, not at all. By the by who told you that?"

"What sir, you are bluffing. Didn't you convey the message to me yesterday night?"

Her words made me livid and with grunted voice I said

"You young lady, what nonsense are you talking? I neither know your phone number nor your house. Sorry, I can't relish such jokes. No kidding with me please".

"Sir, don't tell lie. Yesterday night at 9.30 did you not remember me and felt like talking to me? Tell me honestly?" came the question with all seriousness.

Before I could reply she said Bye and continued her jog making me highly irritated. I continued my walk recollecting the thoughts came into my mind previous night .To my shocking surprise, she was correct. At about 9.30 when I was watching TV a desire to talk to her had flashed in my mind. I was shaken with this coincidence. While sipping the coffee after getting back home, I told my wife the strange experience I had with that lady. She didn't take it seriously, but teased me by telling "You be careful with that damsel. She may be <u>Mohini</u>". Though my wife laughed it of, I could not take it lightly, as it was a strange experience.

Two

I was not well and was not able to go for walk for three days. The fourth day I felt better and stepped out as usual, very much against the wishes of my wife. When I reached the meeting place that lady also arrived, with a difference. In the sense, she was in her blue tracksuit instead of her usual white and was not as charming as she was.

"Sir, Good morning, why you were missing for three days? Were you not well or what?" she asked. Surprisingly, she started walking with me instead of overtaking with a 'Bye'.

"Sir, from today I want to come along with you rather not going me alone; if you don't mind"

"Why? What happened young lady? Are you scared of dogs or what?" was my tickling question.

"Nothing of that sort Sir. Some how I like to join you. That's all. You have no objection, I suppose. One more request sir. Hereafter you don't call me young lady like a stranger. I am Maya Sharma. You can call me Maya."

"It is my pleasure Maya to walk with you and what objection I can have" I said and both of us started walking together.

There was silence for quite sometime which I broke and said "Shall I take the liberty of asking you, Maya, why you are wearing blue track suit instead of your regular beautiful white one, today? "

She laughingly replied "Sir, you are quite naughty! You observe what I wear daily. Sir! today is Amavasya (new moon day) and I don't like Amavasya first of all; so also wearing white dress on this day. Strange! you know, sir?" After a pause she said again "Why sir? Am I not looking good in blue?"

"Nothing like that. I just asked you. Only thing is you look different today." Maya, I have a small doubt. How come Your face will be glowing always? This is something unique.. What face cream you use" I said.

"Uncle! Sorry, Sorry, Sir! you observe so many things. You look at my dress and face only or something else also?" She asked with a mischievous look and quaint smile. I felt embarrassed and said "Sorry"." Sir, don't feel bad. I said just as a joke. The answer to your question is I never use any face cream as I am allergic to these chemicals"

Our walking together became routine .She used to come from the cross road and join me at the meeting place at the same time; walk along for about forty minutes and depart from the same meeting place telling 'Bye'. The time of saying "Bye" used to be not later than 6AM and most of the mornings used to be still dark. Our walk would be with more of reticence and blissful smile of Maya now and then. One thing I was not able to understand was how Maya could join me exactly at the same time even during my late or early arrivals at the meeting place. Twice or thrice I reached the meeting place much early deliberately without informing her in advance. But to my shocking surprise she was there exactly at the same time. Whenever such things happened she commented "Sir, do you think I will not come to know your early start, if you don't tell me?"

"I feel, I have come quite close to you. So, I want to call you "uncle" instead of Sir if you permit" she said one day in the midst of our walk. I gladly gave consent to her and from then on Maya started addressing me as Uncle.

Three

Time had gone on and our acquaintance was for more than four months. Our intimacy levels went up progressively from superficial level to feeling level. We were really close and good friends. We started getting to know each other more personally. I learnt that she was basically from Belgaum married to Sharma and landed in Bangalore about six months back. Her husband a Software engineer was in USA on an assignment and was expected back shortly. She was staying alone with a servant maid and her parents were expected to join her which had not happened from quite some time. She also fairly understood me and my background. Though Maya became close and a good friend, her behavior at times used to be peculiar. One thing I distinctly observed was that she used to be very much hesitant and vague while talking about her family matters. Another surprising thing was in spite of my repeated invitations to visit my house and meet my wife; she didn't make it even once in these four months though she was living alone. It was also a bit strange that Maya never called me to visit her house even as a formality. The most astonishing thing was keeping herself away from me at a distance of minimum three feet at all time and any of my attempts to go closer than that used to be futile. In all, with her odd behavior now and then and uncanny experiences of telepathy I felt her as paranormal many times.

It was cloudy and morning was still dark, when we came to the meeting place to depart to our respective destinations. It started drizzling. As I was having umbrella I told Maya that I would accompany until her house. For my shocking surprise, She vehemently reacted "I don't want anybody to come to my house .I know how to take care of myself. This rain can do nothing to me. You please go back to your house." and rushed towards her house disappearing in no time. I felt affronted and terribly upset with her rude behavior. I immediately decided not to meet her thenceforth.

"I am so sorry uncle. Please join me for the walk. I will give written apology to you. I will be waiting in our meeting place." The words of Maya made me to jump up from the bed. My watch was showing 5AM.Due to my sudden waking up my wife got disturbed and said "What happened? Since yesterday you are not keeping well. You better skip your walk." As I had determined to avoid Maya, I went to sleep again.

The day next to next of the incident I started much early from the house with the intention of not meeting Maya. When I reached the meeting place she was standing there waiting for me. I continued my walk ignoring her, without even wishing her. She followed me and called me with a repentant voice "Yesterday itself I apologized. I thought you would pardon me and join for walk yesterday itself. I once again beg your pardon. Uncle, kindly understand, I was totally disturbed other day. I know you were upset with my behavior. I am a lonely lady; don't give me such big punishment. I hope my uncle is really magnanimous."

I was silently listening to her without any reply continuing my walk. After a long pause I busted out "Maya don't try to appease me by giving stupid reasons. I am repenting for being friendly and affectionate with you. I take this as a grave insult to me. After all, it was a basic courtesy from a cultured person to anybody in that situation. The reaction from you was not expected from any rational human being. I am sorry, that sort of arrogant behavior I can't tolerate from anybody."

She was following me silently and started crying after a few minutes. I could not bear that and asked to join me by telling "you are excused." she was immensely happy and said "Uncle, Thanks a lot" wiping her tears from the hanky. Even, I was in tears for the reason not known. My act of pardoning was for her repentance or my own interest of keeping her intimacy, honestly, I didn't know.

It was the month of September and my wife took North Indian tour along with her brothers and cousins. She was very angry with me as I didn't join her. It was almost a week after she had left. I and Maya were on our usual morning walk.

"Uncle, shall I join for dinner in the night today" Maya asked breaking the silence prevailing for sometime.

"No, dear, my wife is not in station and you have to eat what I cook"

"I know that Aunty is out of station. I will cook for you. Only thing is you have to say OK." was the reply.

There was no other go but to say yes. Also, it was another incomprehensible experience of Maya, how she came to know about my wife's non availability though I had never made a mention about her trip.

I never wanted Maya to cook anything in the house for dinner. So, I prepared some colored rice and curds rice and brought some sweets and fruits from outside. I set right some of the things in the house which were untidy due to my wife's absence. Right from nine my anxious waiting for Maya was on with mixed feelings and crazy thinking. I was so restless that I was moving in and out of the house again and again. Any sound outside, was making me to rush to the gate in the illusion of Maya's arrival. It was almost ten and was terribly boring which made me to switch on the TV. The ringing sound of phone made me to wake up from the nap. As I rushed to the phone to receive the call, it got disconnected. I was feeling miserable and decided to have dinner and moved towards dining table. Immediately I changed my mind to wait for some more time as I was very much hopeful about Maya's arrival. The sweet voice of Maya "Sorry Uncle, I will not be able to join for the dinner .Kindly excuse me" followed by serenade, shook me up from my sleep and made me to run to the window to see nobody. The clock was showing eleven. I was enraged with the fooling trick of Maya and had my dinner with mouthful of cursing.

I had decided to bang Maya next day for her nasty game. As usual she joined me for the walk in the morning in our meeting place. She was very casual and said "Good morning" with no reciprocation from my end. We were walking together silently. I got annoyed at her long silence as I was expecting a deep regret immediately after our meeting in the morning. I shouted "Maya, I never expected that you are so discourteous and ill mannered. OK, you didn't join for dinner. But you didn't have the courtesy to phone up and tell me your inability to join even though you knew my phone no. I am really sorry for your nomadic behavior." But her reaction was very cool.

"Uncle, I know you are angry with me. But it is not right on your part to blame me like this. Did you not hear me telling "Sorry" at eleven? Perhaps you have forgotten as you were not fully awake. Does not matter. I say sorry once again.

Uncle! I remember a quote of Aristotle and I think I must tell you.

'Any one can be angry – that is easy. But to be angry with the right person, to the right degree, at the right time, for the right purpose, and in the right way – this is not easy.'"

I just stopped and was about to thrash her. But, there was a flash in my mind about her voice of regret at eleven previous night. I shivered with that experience and was totally confused.

"Why uncle, am I correct?" she said and we continued our walk. Maya was about to take turn towards her house. I asked her to stop and about to pat her to say "just ignore about my anger". She suddenly said "You mischievous uncle, you want to touch me or what? Don't think of it. You will never be able to do that" with a sarcastic laugh.

Maya! How can you think so mean like that? You know I am fifty eight years and a father like figure. It is my habit to pat a person whenever I feel close and affectionate. It is very bad of you." I said with a sorry figure.

"Oh, uncle, I made a joke. Don't take it seriously. Even if you hug me I don't feel bad. I know you can't do that". I was not able to understand what she meant by that.

"Maya, I want to visit your house soon. I want to talk to you something personal seriously." I told her with the intention of getting more details about her.

"The time will come uncle. I will invite you to my house. You know, I have not settled down fully. My husband is in USA. I am alone here only with my servant maid. My parents who had promised me to join have not joined yet. Also I have no phone connection. Anyway I will call you soon and host a grand candle light dinner. Uncle! You will have a surprise gift also.

Anyway I show my house from here. But, Uncle! Don't venture to come to my house till I call you."

Immediately I said "What will you do if I come"

"Uncle! You will miss a great thing in your life! that is me."

She showed me a house with blue color which was almost at the end of the cross road and bid "Bye". The house was not clearly visible as the morning was not bright.

Four

Day by day Maya was becoming complex and also a disturbing element. Her unusual behavior in various incidents was increasing and telepathic experiences became very frequent. Many times I was frightened with her bizarre acts of telepathy. I was waiting for the earliest opportunity to ask her thread bare about her factual background.

"Maya, I want to talk to you frankly certain things today. I don't bother whether you like it or not." told her with all seriousness in the midst of our walk one day. She immediately stopped and stared at me with a mesmerizing smile. She was gorgeous and sparkling even in the dim light of street lamps. I was dumb founded and became totally blank after seeing her. I simply said "Maya! You are so beautiful. I don't know how a human can be so beautiful?".

With a wild laugh she said "You wanted to say I am beautiful? To say this you made that blab, blab uncle?"

Uncle! You are just seeing me in my track suit and in darkness. I don't know how you feel if you see me in moon light with my traditional dress on.

Uncle! You know? I used to be called as Beladingala Bale (Moon light girl) in my college days". There was a silence for sometime.

How is that you are becoming romantic? Uncle. Hannele is

chiguring (The old yellow leaf is growing greener)?" I felt bad with her teasing words.

"What do you mean by that Maya? Just because I am fifty eight, I should not appreciate beauty? Is it?

It is not the age that decides one's ability to enjoy beauty. It is a person's Zest for life is the deciding factor which I have in abundance still."

"I didn't mean like that uncle. I just said if you become more romantic it would be problematic to you only, especially now, that aunty is away."

"Maya, you are not just beautiful, but, taunting too"

By the time our conversation ended, we were near our meeting place and we dispersed.

Ridiculously, I was infatuated and started thinking always about Maya after her electrifying look of that day. My mind was full of Maya's smile, Maya's eyes and Maya and nothing else. The eagerness to see Maya in moon light turned agonizing. It was more than a week. I was totally restless and opened up one morning and said

"Maya, even if you think me shameless I don't mind. Please tell me when I will have the look of True Maya?"

In fact, I was expecting her resentment if not her vehement reply. After a long pause she whispered with a smile "Uncle, it can happen whenever you want. But, you may not see me anymore after that."

I didn't understand what she meant and with a big laugh I said "How can it happen? Maya can never leave me and go. She is my best and close friend."

There was no reply from her and after a while she said "Uncle, today is Tuesday and the next Monday is 'Adbhut Poornima' (wonderful full moon day). On that day I will be visiting Annapoorneshwari temple in the night along with my few selected friends for special pooja. I will be passing in front of your house between 10.30 and 11PM. You can definitely see me in my traditional dress on that night; of course, if you sincerely want to? Uncle! My request to you is, you neither come nearer nor talk to me on that night, if you see me. The reason being I am not supposed to talk till I finish my pooja and back home."

"Maya, you have not seen my house and say you would pass through my house. I hope you are not kidding?"

"Just because I have not visited your house, you think I don't know? I will be passing through your house very often especially in the nights and also seen you many times standing near the gate. Perhaps you might not have identified me."

"Hay,Maya, I have heard so many Poornimas but not heard of Adbhuta poornima. Can you tell me what is it's significance"

"Uncle don't ask too many questions. I will not be able to answer and I only want your assurance that you would not talk to me during that time. OK! Regarding Poornima better ask Aunty when she comes back."

By that time we were back in the meeting place. Maya said "Bye" and left the place though I was wanting to talk for some more time.

Five

The D-Day, the Adbhuta Poornima started with a big disappointment, as Maya didn't join for the morning walk. I consoled myself thinking her to be busy in preparing for Pooja.I was restless right from morning in the eagerness of seeing Beladingala Bale. I finished my dinner in a hurry, as I was not relishing .I came to portico at 9.30 itself craving for the look of real Maya. As the night was getting wilder the moon was rising gradually towards pinnacle spilling the pleasant light all over, as if to combat the cruelty of darkness. It was10.30 and I was in total turmoil with anxiety and apprehensions swirling around. I was feeling as if my eyes had come to stand still for not taking chance of missing that unknown beauty even for a moment. It was 11 o'clock and the sky was totally milky with the moon brightest in the middle. There were no indications of Maya's arrival and shadows of disappointment started setting in. An emotional conflict arouse with my mind telling 'too much hope deceiveth' and heart believing 'Hope is brightest when it dawns from fears'.

When I looked at my watch it was showing 11.15 and all my hopes to see Maya came to cold. I decided to go to bed thinking Maya to be a big cheat. As I was about to close the door, the sound of chanting mantras was heard which made me to rush to the gate like mad with heart palpitating.

Oh! God! It was incredible; amidst the group of five beautiful ladies was Maya the most beautiful, in her milky white sari with long hairs and diamond studs in her ears shining and the radiant eyes reflecting Moon light. She was an abode of divine beauty and "Beladingala Bale" to the core .My eyes welled up with tears of joy. Maya stopped in front of my house momentarily as if to make me understand 'what really beauty is '. Though I was tempted very much to go nearer to have a closer look of that celestial beauty, the promise I had made to Maya held me in thrall. She walked away and disappeared imprinting the bliss in my indelible memory.

I was standing near the gate gauging the vacuum created by the disappearance of Maya. Madness, cowering in the chill of full moon day I was praying God, to grace the look of that blissful beauty at least for one more time. The chirping sound of a flock of white cranes flying in the sky brought me to senses and I went inside. I was lying on the bed in a strange state of mind. 'My emotional mind was telling Maya to be a celestial body and not human, though my rational mind was not prepared to accept'

As psychologists say 'our emotions have a mind of their own, one which can hold views quite independently of our rational mind."

The Adbhuth Poornima ended in a real wonderful way with all my agonies turning to ecstatic moments.

I was the man who always disagrees with the opinion of two separate identities of Sex and Beauty as far as woman is concerned. I always pleaded that Sex and Beauty are synonymous and there is nothing like Beauty without sex and sex without beauty. But, the transcending beauty of Maya I witnessed topsy turvied my opinion. That was true happiness in the disguise of beauty with not a tint sex in it. There was no other rational reason not to accept"Beauty is God". It was my heart that saw Maya and not my eyes.

'It is with heart that one see rightly, what is essential is invisible to the eyes"

"Not like earthly beauty dangerous to look upon, but like the morning star which is thy (God's) emblem, bright and musical, breathing purity, telling of heaven and infusing peace"   --- Bible.

Six

had sleepless night almost. I started early in the morning and reached the meeting place much before my usual time in the anxiety and excitement of meeting Maya to express my feelings. She was not there. Thinking that she would be late due to late night Pooja, I decided to wait for some time. It was almost half an hour and Maya didn't turn up. Totally disappointed, I went back home instead of continuing the walk. To my great dismay she didn't come for walk for four days causing concern. I felt many times to visit her house to enquire her welfare. But her words "Uncle, don't venture to come to my house till I call you. Otherwise you are going to loose a great thing in life that is me" virtually scared me and made me to abstain from doing that. Days turned to weeks with no trace of Maya and not even her telepathic messages. My growing anxiety turned to restlessness and I decided to visit her house at any cost. It was Saturday, around10AM I went in search of the Blue house, which she had shown, from a distance. When I reached that house, the gate was locked. My knocking of the gate and calling for Maya yielded no response and had to come back frustrated. The next day being Sunday, hoping against hopes of seeing Maya I went to that house again. It was same thing with door locked. As my tension was unbearable I went to next house to enquire thinking that they might have some information about her. The reply from the gentleman next door "There is nobody staying in this house by name Maya Sharma. In fact the house is vacant for the past six months and the owner is in Dubai. The house key is with me only. He has asked me to look for a good tenant for renting out." was diabolic and made me to rush back home shivering. Subsequently, I visited every house almost in that road enquiring for Maya thinking that I mistook the house she had shown; with no avail. My wife's words "You be careful with that damsel. She may be **Mohini**" started haunting in my mind. The loneliness besides mystery of missing Maya made me delirious. I was forlorn at Maya's act of desertion. I stopped my morning walk as I developed a sort of agoraphobia (fear of open space).

I was relieved to a great extent when my wife returned from her long tour of 45 days. She felt bad after seeing my plight

"Why are you looking so sick? Were you not eating properly in my absence? I told you many times to go to your brother's house regularly for food. I know you have not done that." was her series of questions. I was silent as the reason was not that and was totally different. Next day when she got up I was on the bed awake. She was surprised and asked me "Why? What happened? You have stopped your morning walk or what?

I simply said "Yes".

"Any unpleasant incident with your girl friend Maya?" was her next question with a quaint accent .At that moment I felt like telling Maya's episodes in her absence. The apprehension of her mistaking the incidents prevented me from doing so. I kept mum.

It was again a full moon day after a month. I came to portico after my dinner, looking at the moon recollecting the celestial experience of Adbhut poornima. This poornima was a real "Nirasha Poornima (Disappointing Full moon day)" in stark contrast to the previous one, lifeless, without the appearance of Maya. The call of my wife informing the time as eleven made me to come to senses. I went inside with heavy heart.

"Uncle, I am so sorry. I should not have done that. I had to go in a hurry without informing you. I had summons from the far off place. I know you are too much upset. I also know you can very well understand my problem.

Come on Uncle! I am back and will be with you forever. Resume your walk. Get up fast, I will be waiting in our usual meeting place." the musical voice of Maya startled me and made me to leap from the bed .I started looking for Maya all around. After sometime I could realize that it was not Maya but her telepathic voice. My heart was pounding with joy in anticipation of meeting Maya after a long gap. I got ready and left the house as before. My wife was fast asleep.

I reached the meeting place in high spirits to see Maya and burst out all the feelings I was holding for the past one month. Her absence was disheartening and every minute of waiting was increasingly painful. There was no trace of her even after half an hour which drove me crazy and I started crying loudly. I decided to return home in disgust and turned back

Suddenly, I heard the sound of wild laugh followed by a sweet voice "Uncle" which made me to turn back.

Oh, God! It was my Maya there with her White track suit on. It was unbelievable .My eyes were shedding tears of joy and I was totally dumb founded.

"Uncle, You want to continue walk or stand here just looking at me? Her words made me conscious and the joy of sight of Maya turned to anger.

"You Maya the cruel lady, where were you all these days? How can you vanish without informing me. I am feeling like hitting you" I said and lifted the batten I was carrying.

"Uncle ! Uncle! Halt." She shouted and stared at me .The flash of her look and the mesmerizing voice turned me to statue like and I stood with my raised hand unmoved. Maya looking at my plight, came a little closer to me I became totally wet with sweat and shivering set in that chilly morning.

"Uncle, shun your anger, it is not good for health. Come on, let us move and continue our walk. "As she said that, my hand came down automatically and I began to walk behind her slowly. I was speechless and was following her like a pet dog following his master.

After about ten minutes, I broke the silence and resumed my talk in shrill and shivering voice. I was highly emotional.

"Maya, why you play such tricks? You don't know how much I am attached to you and how deserted will be without seeing you.

Maya, you please tell me who are you?

From that night of adhbhut poornima, I am very much scared of you."

Interrupting my breathless talk, there was a flashing reply

"Why Uncle? Was I looking so scary? I thought you would be appreciating me.   I am really disappointed. Uncle, I have already told you the reason why I was away from you."

" Maya, it is not like that. You are not just beautiful. You are a celestial beauty and super natural. I think my wife is right. You are not Maya! You are "MOHINI"

"Uncle, please stop that crazy thinking. I am neither Mohini nor Rohini. I am just Maya Sharma."

Suddenly, a black dog appeared from nowhere and started barking at us. I was shocked with its appearance and chased it way with my batten. It looked, Maya was bit shaken. Our walk continued but, silence hovered again.

A stupid idea popped up and I jumped forward towards her to hold her hand who was about 5 to 6 feet away from me. I stumbled and was about to fall down. Fortunately, I didn't.

"Uncle, I have told many times, You can't touch me, still you tried and this is the result" she said with sarcastic laugh.

"OK! You want to know who I am. You don't want to believe that I am Maya Sharma?"

By the time she said that we were near our point of depart.

'"Uncle, I am sorry, it is time to leave. Uncle, t his time it is not Bye. It's Good Bye" She deviated towards her house.

"Maya! Maya!" My shouting was not heard and I became total blank and felt suffocated. I came to stand still and closed my eyes. After sometime I felt a push and slowly opened my eyes. My breathing became normal. My search for Maya was in vain. Though I was prompted to go in search of her to her house I didn't dare do it. I was slowly moving towards my house and the sky was getting brighter indicating the rising of Sun to bring the world to light. The early morning breeze which was mild and fragrant turned wild at once to dusty wind. In the whirl of the wind a sheet of paper came flying and stuck to my face. I tried to read the matter in it with no avail due to the absence of spects and insufficient light. I kept it in my pocket and reached home.

I was sipping my second cup of morning coffee, and my mind was full of Maya's thoughts. I was in confusion about revealing my meet with Maya to Sudha. As I had the last sip, suddenly remembered the sheet of paper and took out from pocket.

Oh, God! The letter was of Maya with glittering gold letters. It read "Uncle, you visit the following address and you will know who I am" It contained

Belgaum address with no name of person.

"Sudha, come here fast and bring a cup of water too" my frightened voice made her to rush to the room. She was shocked to see me shivering with the paper in my hand.

"What happened? Whose letter is that? Drink water first please."

She made me to drink forcibly. I held her hands tight and showed that sheet of paper to her after a while. She was not able to understand anything about the address written in that letter. As I calm down, I slowly narrated the spine chilling experience of Maya in the morning. I also told her the strange experiences of Maya I had during her absence including her appearance on Adhbhut Poornima. Night..

"On that day itself I hinted her as Mohini. But you didn't believe.

Enough is enough. Now on, don't even think of your morning walks" was her categorical ruling and that made me to keep on hold my morning walks from then on.

Seven

It was more than two weeks and life was becoming untenable with no morning strolls and no constructive work of any sort. I was in total emotional turmoil, always thinking about the address given by Maya and the mystery behind it. At the same time I was not wanting to take unilateral decision to visit Belgaum against the wishes of Sudha. Amidst these emotional clashes I was sinking a bit by bit.

"Uncle, why you stopped your morning walks? Are you really afraid of seeing me?

Uncle, when are you visiting Belgaum to know my details. You were always asking me who I am? Now I have given the details, but, you are not visiting.

Come on, uncle; I am back. Cheer up" the scintillating voice of Maya awakened and I got up in shock. It was 4.45 AM and Sudha was in deep sleep. I firmed up my mind to proceed for walk and when I stepped out with jogging shoes and batten in hand it was 5.15 AM. Thank God! Sudha was not disturbed and she was engrossed in her sleep. After a gap of almost 20 days, I was feeling jittery as I started moving. With my heart pounding and mind full of fear, I reached the meeting place. I expected Maya to be there, but she was not. I looked around for her presence, with no trace of her. In dilemma, whether to wait or to come back,I was restless. Finally, after a wait of twenty minutes, I turned to start back. Suddenly, there was a flash of energy in my body and I was pushed forward. In full enthusiasm I resumed my walk with the feel of Maya beside with her occasional piercing look; but no Maya in existence.

When I reached home Sudha was sitting on door step anxiously waiting for my return. She was furious and the argument we entered into turned to virtual quarrel. With that unsavoury happening, I decided to put an end to my morning walks.

My restlessness doubled with a feel of treachery and I decided to discuss with Sudha to bring an end with a visit to Belgaum. It was Thursday morning and an unusual thought of visiting Temple came to my mind .After my bath, I took my Activa and went straight to Srinidhi temple. I didn't inform Sudha as she was in bath room. We were sitting face to face to have our lunch and straight away I raised the topic of visiting Belgaum to brake the mystery of Maya and also to know the facts. The conversation went well and consensus arrived without much problems. We both agreed to take Sujaya our relative who has an uncle a resident of Belgaum.

When we arrived, it was 6.30 in the morning and we were received with a big smile by Nagaraj (Sujaya's uncle) in the Bus station. We proceeded to his house in his car. As all the three of us were exhausted due to bus journey, there was no much conversation. I was much more tired due to disturbed sleep arouse by the pop ups of Maya's thoughts throughout the journey. Around nine all of us were at the dining table and I briefed the purpose of our fact finding mission. In fact, Nagaraj was not ready to believe my experiences and ridiculed our purpose of visit in spite of my showing the paper containing the message. Suma, Nagaraj's wife served the sumptuous breakfast and only three of us decided to visit the " House of Unknown" leaving Sujaya and Suma at home. We left the house at 10.45 with Nagaraj at the steering. As the car was speeding up my heart was thumping with the blood gushing in the veins. Every beat of my heart was sounding Maya and every thought in my mind was a flash of mystic Maya.

Eight

At 11.30 the car stopped in front of a house looking to be big with huge compound but, with faded and discolored exterior indicating " Everything is not really well". The name plate was showing the name   "Anantha Sharma" and the address written as No.17,Gandhi colony, the one we were looking for. With much hesitation and apprehension I opened the gate and moved slowly towards the main door with Nagaraj and Sudha behind. After the third ring of calling bell the door was opened carefully by a person in late fifties. There was a simple "hello" for my introduction of myself as "Murthy from Bangalore". As Nagaraj entered into the scene with his introduction as Asst. commissioner of Sales tax and a localities, there was a welcome into the house. There was silence and my mind was working actively for different alternatives to start the topic. Finally, I broke the pause

"Sir! Please don't mistake me. Sir! You have daughter by name Maya? When I said that in all hesitation, Anant looked at his wife Anjana. Suddenly, she got up from the sofa and went inside crying. Sudha seeing that followed her to the room.

"Sir, I am so sorry. My idea of asking was not to hurt you." I said apologetically and narrated in length my exhilarating experiences with Maya and the mystery of getting his address. Anant was shivering with Maya's letter in hand. With tears rolling down he shared the heart rending tragedy of his life that is "the pathetic end of his only daughter Chaaya Sharma"

Anant Sharma is the Asst.Commissioner,Sales tax from Belgaum, well to do with comfortable living. Anjana his very co operative wife and Chaaya the only daughter ,a girl very cute and charming. She being the only kid was brought up with lots of love and care. After completion of her schooling, she joined one of the best colleges of Belgaum and came out with a degree in Commerce. Her growing age in conjunction with her enhancing beauty turned her into "Beladingala Baale"(as she used to be called in her college) by end of her teen. In Anant's words "her growing beauty with her growing age was a matter of growing concern for parents". She took up a job in a company very much against the wishes of parents. She being jaunty ,jovial and zooming became very popular in the company in a working span of six months. She was very fond of driving and used to go for long drives with her friends taking Papa's car. Many times there were virtual quarrels between father and daughter concerning Chaaya's rash and Speedy driving. Among many of her friends, Udai was close and a family friend who used to visit her house often. Also, there was a friendship at family level.

It was Saturday and half a day at office for Chaaya. She came home and went straight to her room without proper response to Anjana's offer for coffee which was unusual. The sound of shutting the doors was an indication of her disturbed mind. Chaaya joined Anant and Anjana at the dining table around 9PM .Ananat looking at her dull face sensed fishy and asked " My dear. What is wrong?. You are OK?"

"Papa, I am alright. But, there is one thing worrying me and I don't know how to put it" was the reply.

"Beta, don't worry. Tell us what is in your mind."

Chaaya, a bold and out spoken, immediately responded " I want to marry Udai."

Anant and Anjana were shaken and they became speechless.

After a few minutes Chaaya breaking the silence "Papa, this is not the decision and only proposal and can happen only with your consent."

"Dear daughter, you have put us in affray. Please give us sometime to think. For heaven sake don't do anything in haste and land in trouble. This is my request."

Anant's strained words put her into deep emotions. Chaaya got up from her chair and in the deep embrace of Anant said "Papa, I never do anything that hurts you"

Udai, a smart and handsome with a descent family background. In other words, he was a good match to Chaaya in all respects except for his caste, a lingayat. Anant though not very orthodox, a proud Brahmin. After long and prolonged discussions and consultations Anant and Anjana decided to meet the parents of Udai with regard to the marriage of Chaaya and Udai.

Thank God! Without major hurdles things went in favor of marriage and   there was consent from both sides. The marriage took place in a fairly grand scale with the presence of majority of friends and relations from both sides. Though the marriage was one of compromise, Anant and Anjana were really happy as it was Chaaya's choice of her life partner

Nine

The wheel of time was rolling ahead and in the course of it, as an envy of destiny, a havoc was in offing for the Anants who were in the pinnacle of happiness. It was just about two months of her marriage; one evening Chaaya came home straight from office, giving a pleasant surprise to Anjana. She was looking dull, but Anjana felt that was due to her exhaustion in office. While having her cup of coffee Chaaya said "Amma,I want to stay back tonight here and go to office in the morning". In fact, that was Anjana's wishes also. Unlike other days, Chaaya was lying on the bed in her room ,who always used to be with Mom yapping, yapping yapping. Anant got disturbed to see Chaaya dull and pale during dinner and asked Anjana to find the reason.

Chaaya's words "Amma, will you sleep with me tonight in my room, I am feeling very lonely" were really shocking to Anjana and Chaaya was awake with crying and sobbing the whole night. In the morning, suspecting some problem, both Ananat and Anjana tried hard to reason out with no avail. For all their questions, the answers from her was positive, but, they smelt a rat about the strained relationship of Chaaya and Udai.

Gradually, Chaaya's staying at her parents house was becoming frequent and also Udai's visit to Anant's house was very much reduced. With these developments the suspicion of Anants about the deepening differences between Chaaya and Udai started surfacing out Anjana specially was a worried woman .It was a week day afternoon , Chaaya came home crying skipping the office putting Anjana to her shock of life. There was no proper answer for series of questions of her. Anant arrived in a hurry after hearing Chaaya's abrupt arrival, over the phone. When he entered the room with Anjana , Chaaya was lying in her bed with her eyes full of tears. Both sitting on either side and with touching voice started enquiring about her problems. After a lot persuasion Chaaya put them in swirl by saying "Papa,I cannot live anymore with Udai and need separation" Her word of divorce was bolt from the blue for Anant & Anjana ,a couple known to be ideal and roll model in their family circle. With all the care and caution, they consoled and advised her not to jump into conclusions and think thoroughly on the drastic steps. Next day morning she went back with heavy heart. For quite sometime there was neither a phone call nor a visit from Chaaya which consoled them to some extent with a thought of patch up of relations between Chaaya and Udai.

The sound of calling bell made Anjana to wake up from her afternoon nap. The appearance of Chaaya with two suit cases ,when she opened the door was no less than the strike of thunderbolt. Chaaya entered silently and walked straight to her room. This time there were no tears in her eyes but look of a determined decision. After freshening up, she joined mother in kitchen and with a cup of coffee in her hand "Amma! I am back into my house totally liberated. I will never go back to that butchery. I hope, you people won't mind".

The stream of rolling tears from her radiant eyes was an indication of the depth of agony she was undergoing.

"Papa, I change my favorite slogan of my life "**I hate tears**" to **"I like tears"**. Do you know why? Papa.

Here on tears are the solace for my aching heart."

The heart rending words of Chaaya at dinner time shattered Anant totally and he hugged her tightly. The sound of his cry was resounding echoing the whole house.

Ten

Initially, the role of Prabhudev and Manjula the parents of Udai, was suspected behind Chaaya's decision. But their sincere efforts to prevent the disaster was a clear indication of their non involvement of any sort. Also, there was no grouse of any kind against them either,by Chaaya. The repeated attempts and countless counseling both by her and Udai's parents yielded no positive results. Though Udai showed some inclination for compromise, Chaaya was firm in her decision to go for the ultimate and never heeded to pressures of any sort. .She went to the extent of telling Anjana that she would go away and live separately if they try to persuade the matter further. The shocking thing for both the families was that none of the reasons given by Chaaya was justified for such extreme step. Whatever, the truth behind Chaaya's diabolic decision remained as a mystery for everyone but for Udai and Chaaya. Finally, what should not have happened, happened and Chaaya's "Love marriage". for love turned contrast. Her relationship with Udai ended ultimately with a legal Divorce. and came to an end.

Chaaya switched over to other company mainly to avoid Udai. Her new office was quite far from Anant's house which made her to use Papa's car for commuting .As the days and months were passing on the agonizing memories of her past were fading gradually. At the same time, Anant and Anjana were getting worried about her future.

Many of their attempts to convince Chaaya for her re- marriage turned futile with her categorical rejection. The jaunty jovial girl turned to a shaky, morose and lifeless lady in a year's time. The visible descent of Beladingala Baale" to a lack luster appearence was the depiction of the deep rooted damage caused due to the devastating event of her life. She was in total dark about her future with no idea whatsoever .But destiny had already planned a dirty game against her.

It was Saturday and Chaaya got ready to go to office. Some how, she was dull and sluggish with a sick look.

"Chaaya,you are looking to be not well. Why don't you apply leave and take rest

at home" were the words of Anjana.

"No ,Amma ,I am OK. Any way today is Saturday and I will be coming early.

Amma , let us go to a movie in the evening and will have dine out. Don't prepare any Khana for the night. Also tell Papa about this programme." She replied and started the car. With a long wave, she zoomed towards the office. Alas! Neither of them thought that would be the last wave and Good bye to life by Chaaya.

Anant was back home early by 5 PM after knowing the evening programme from Anjana, but surprised to see the absence of daughter .In fact, he was very happy about her decision of outing as he wanted her to be as happy as possible and come out of the emotional malaise. The continued delay of Chaaya's arrival was causing too much of anxiety and Anjana was cursing her for not communicating the delay. With the dark sky outside and no response to their phone call, both of them were became restless and were worried. It was 7.30 and the ringing sound of phone made Anant to rush for it.

"Is this Chaaya's residence please" the unfamiliar voice surprised him.

" Yes, who is speaking" was his reply

"This is Inspector Asohk and want to speak to Chaaya's father or any other senior person". The word Inspector made Anant jittery and asked"What is the matter inspector? is everything OK with Chaaya? I am her father" he said.

"Sir, you come immediately to KR Hospital without delay. I will tell the details later" the words of Ashok made him to shout "Anju! Come fast, let us go" .As they reached the hospital in half an hour,the eagerly waiting Ashok rushed them to ICU. When both entered, Chaaya was gasping for breath. The shivering voice of her mother "Chaaya,Chaaya, this is your Amma. Please open your eyes" made her to open her eyes. But, that was only for a minute and closed after seeing Anjana and Anant Chaaya closed her eyes once and for all making the eyes of Anant and Anjana wet for ever.

Chaaya had a ghastly accident of crashing her car against a tree while overtaking a truck.

She bid "Adieu" to this materialistic world at the peak of her youth at twenty four, in the year 2002. Of course, the ordeal of Chaaya ended, but her natural desires and ambitions remained unfulfilled.

Eleven

All of us were in the world of Chaaya hearing her tragic travel of shortened life with dried eyes and no tears left to shed. The call of Anant from the stair case made us conscious and we joined him in the first floor .He opened the lock of a room mentioning it Chaaya's and took us inside showing various articles of her including some toys of her childhood. Suddenly, my attention was drawn to a photo hanging on the wall.

Gosh! That was my Maaya!

I didn't know what happened to me? When I opened my eyes, I was lying on Chaaya's bed with all the people surrounding with anxiety. I slowly got up shouted "" Chaaya is my Maya, Chaaya is my Maya" and hug Anant tightly. With heavy heart we left cahaaya's house around 3 PM and reached Nagaraj's house. I was carrying my Maaya in disguise of Chaaya's photo which I took from Anant before I left his house.

We were back in Bangalore immediately, very much against the wishes of Mrs.& Mr.Nagaraj who wanted us to be there for few more days. Though we were back home, we were finding it difficult to come out of shock created by Chaaya/Maya episode .It was more than a month or so, I never stepped out of house at odd hours let alone the morning walks. This was mainly for two reasons; the first being the fear of appearance of Maya and its consequences and the other being the strict instructions of Sudha for not taking any chance .Also ,there were no instances of any Strange happenings or experiences of Maya.

"Uncle! Why you stopped your morning walk? Is it because you have come to know who I am .Uncle, Without your company I am feeling lonely for the past month and a half. Please join me at our meeting place." The call of Maya after a considerable gap made me to jump up from bed. I was shivering and sweating. This made Sudha to get up. She switched on the main light rushed, to get me a cup of water. I told her about Maaya,s call for walk and insisted that I should meet her. She was very much angry and was very much against me going out.. After a lengthy argument she accepted with a condition that she would join me for the walk. Both of us moved out of the house at 5.15 after freshening up I was carrying the baton and also the big torch and Sudha an idol of Lord Hanuman. She was totally scared and was continuously chanting Mantras We reached our usual meeting place to find no Maaya there. We were waiting with anxiety and fear and Sudha shivering violently inspite her thick shawl. In fact she was standing with her eyes closed and chanting of Mantras was getting louder. I was looking around with the torch on. My watch was showing ten minutes to Six and returned home in disgust. Sudha was completely shaken and was in total silence till we reached home.

"Uncle, why you brought Aunty? Are you really scared me or what? Am I looking so scary for you? Come alone.

With a pause she continued "Don't worry, Aunty will not get up. Don't disturb her, It is getting late." This time the voice was a bit harsh. I woke up and saw Sudha in deep sleep with snoring. I came out and was feeling energetic and confident.

"Oh God! Maya in her white track suit with her flashing eyes was sighted at the meeting place. I became dumb founded and stood staring at her. The tears of joy was rolling out from my eyes and was confused to understand the figure in front me was whether Maya or Chaaya.

"Uncle, what happened? Come on, it is getting late. Let us move"

This time I was behind Maya moving slowly instead side by side. I was silent and enjoying her heavenly smile she was giving now and then on the way.

"Uncle, I am getting bored. Why are you not speaking? I always liked your manly voice "

I was not able to speak though I wanted, as the look of Maaya after a gap of almost two months created a sort of emotional swirl in my mind.

"Uncle" the raised voice of her. Shook me up and I came to stand still.

"Uncle, it is getting late. I have to go. My request to you is please join me   at 4.30 AM tomorrow.. Uncle, please note, alone. I have to share some secret of my life, which I couldn't, even do with my mother.

Uncle, after that I will not meet for ever and will never trouble any more " Her movements became faster. Suddenly, I got spirited

"Maaya, Please stop. Don't run away. I have a question for you. Tell me Maaya,

You are from Belgaum and you had never seen me before. You want to share the secret which you have not revealed to your parents even .Why is that so and what is so special about me?"

She started laughing and gave a sarcastic look and said," You get answer for all your doubts tomorrow. Uncle, 4.30, tomorrow, alone" In a flash of a moment she vanished. I kept on shouting "Maaya,Maaya." It was 6 when I came home. Sudha was waiting at the door and I had mouthful from her.

Thank God! I managed to keep her away from questioning about Maya.

Twelve

The whole day I was lying on the bed thinking about next day's meeting with Maaya and its after effects. With great difficulty I went into sleep by midnight. Unusually, Sudha was fast asleep by eleven. I opened my eyes in shock and it was 3.30AM.I got ready with my walking dress with baton and an idol of Lord Hanuman. Sudha was in deep sleep which I was not able to understand whether it was natural or Maaya's effect. Also, I made it a appoint to carry the door key. When I came out at 4.15 AM the sky was bright with moon light though it was not Poornima(Full moon day).The pleasant morning breeze made me enthusiastic and energetic. As I was approaching our meeting point my mind was turning to hallucinogenic with strange and fearful thoughts. I suddenly got spirited and I was in front of Maaya .The Maaya I was witnessing was Maaya of Adbhuth Poornima with divinely beauty with a difference in dress. She was with white track suit instead of the traditional heavenly saree.

"Thank you Uncle, for having honoured my words. I am very happy to see you at this hour" The time was exactly 4.30 AM. We started moving slowly in our usual route. After a silence of few minutes, Maya broke the silence with her sweet voice.

"Uncle , first let me apologize for having lied that my husband is in USA. At that time it was required. And which you understand very well. Now you know everything about me,my marriage and so called husband. What I am telling now. Is the bare truth behind my broken marriage with Udai which I kept as secret for obvious reasons. Uncle, my request to you is to keep that secret as secret and let it remain as eternal secret.

Uncle, you have heard the details of me and my marriage from my Dad. Udai, is real smart man and trapped me in his love. The love what I used to dream used to be extraordinarily romantic and the sex that would follow would be the seventh heaven. For my shocking surprise, it turned to be one of torture and suffering from the day one. Udai, who was looking lovable and romantic, was beastly and sadistic. In the nights his acts in the bed used to be barbaric and inhuman. He was a perverse and a molester and not a lover. I finally understood that Udai was a psychopath with no empathy of any sort. My efforts to take him to psychiatrist went unheeded. In one word, I was a spouse of a wife batterer.

Uncle, you can't even imagine what my plight was. I was like a fish out of water, neither keep it to myself nor share with others, my pain of agonizing conjugal relationship with Udai.

Uncle, you can even see some of the marks on my body of his inhuman acts. Finally I decided to come out of the hell created by him and took divorce

I was moving with her silently side by side looking at her glowing face now and then.

"Uncle. my dream of love and fantasies of marital life ,all turned nightmarish.   Chaaya remained alone starving for true love."

"Maya,I am getting tired, I want to rest for sometime"

" No Uncle, You can't do that. I got to go. Don't worry .You will be alright." As she said that, I had a peculiar feeling in my body and I was energized and became fresh..

"Are you OK Uncle? Shall I answer the questions you had asked, now?" She asked and continued.

"Uncle, Destiny played a cruel role both during living and also after. Now you know everything about my life and the end. After death, my destiny turned me to Mohini keeping all humanly desires alive, evocating me to look for a good human to fulfill my desires and denying the eternal peace to my soul.”

There was a pause and Mohini stared at me with a smile.

Oh, God! What a smile? It was a mark of Divine beauty. My eyes were filled with tears of joy.

“Uncle, why are looking like that? Hear me. I Will answer your questions.

You asked me multiple questions like ‘ I am from Belgaum , I had never seen you earlier ,What is so special about me etc. Here is my answer.

“Murthy Uncle” When she said, I was puzzled as Maaya had never called me by name

Uncle, I am Mohini and You must have understood my realm and realities by this time. You know, I am Omni present with my existence everywhere with no limits and bounds. I am also omniscient knowing everything and much more.

Regarding my choice of yours, I was looking for certain qualities in a person to move with and to share with. I was misconceived by his looks and made the wrong choice.. I chose Udai and suffered.. The virtues, features and fondle feelings which were missing in Udai , am finding in you. Also, Murthy Uncle, you are physically fit and mentally strong and I am sure you would dissolve my desires and make way for my Soul to proceed for eternal.

This time I am in no way wrong and you are the best and the right choice. I have decided to be in you and with you for ever “

I suddenly stopped and was shivering.

“Murthy Uncle, don’t be scared. I am no evil spirit. I am your Chaaya and do no harm to you. I will be in you as a driving spirit boosting your energy and morale.”

By the time she concluded, we were at our point of depart and She disappeared.

Immediately, I felt a shove as if somebody pushed me forward. For a moment I became blind and breathless and experienced all the pangs of suffocation. A few minutes later I felt the tender touch of broad palm upon my back and mystic voice resounded in my ears "Uncle, Good Bye. You will not see me any more. But, I am with you and with you always." A queer feeling set in my body and my mind making me extremely joyous; the joy I had experienced on Adbhuth Poornima day after seeing Maya. I started moving forward rigorously with high energy level, in an atmosphere filled with air sweet to breathe and the sky bright with moon light of full moon day associated with a feeling of Maya by the side with her occasional smiles..

When I reached home fresh and cheerful it was 6AM. The main door was still closed. When the door was opened it was strange to see Sudha still sleeping. Immediately, I realized that was Maya's effect. I was anxiously waiting for her to get up and narrated in detail Maya's eternal depart. She started cursing herself for her bad sleep .and her inability to stop me from that morning walk. I kept laughing to myself at Maaya's magical trick on her.

We decided to perform Satyanarayana Pooja and invite Anant & Anjana and Nagaraj & Suma. The pooja went well with pomp and pious. The presence of those people from Belgaum gave a lot of satisfaction to both of us. The unique thing I noticed during pooja was a sort of expression of happiness and gratitude from the face of Chaaya in the photo which I had kept by the side of God's idol. The photo I had collected from Anant and kept in my cupboard and never taken out till that day.

"Murthy Uncle, thanks for the pooja which will give me eternal peace and special thanks for having invited my parents" The tearful and emotional voice of Maya made me to get up. I proceeded for walk with the expectation of meeting Maya again. She was not there, but the feel of her presence and lilt of her celestial voice was there all along my walk.

My morning walk continued without much interruption, but, with a change then on. That is, with neither Maya by the side nor her mysterious musings, instead, an imbuing spirit inside.

After a gap of almost two years Swaroop came down to India during his Semester break to stay with us for a month. We had never spoken to him about my experience of Maya or our visit to Belgaum. The reason was obvious. It was almost two weeks after his arrival and both me and Sudha were in dilemma and undecided about informing him about Maya's episode. It was around 8PM, Sudha was making ready for Dinner and I was sitting in front of TV. Swaroop came down in a hurry with a photo in hand and went straight to Sudha and asked "Whose photo is this? So beautiful and I had never seen this before. Are you planning for my marriage or What?". She was shocked to see Chaaya's photo and directed him to me hesitantly. .After a thorough thought I felt apt and narrated my hair raising experiences of Chaaya/Maya, start to finish from Maya's first meet to the episode of depart. He was terrified and was not prepared to believe. He repeatedly asked "Papa! Whatever you have told is it true?" Next morning, I was not able to go for walk as it was too late when we went to bed.

When I came out at 5.15AM, I was not in my usual mood and started moving with Swaroop by the side. As we were on the go, I was explaining the strange experiences I used to have with Maya and showing certain eventful spots like our meeting place, the spot where I had strange feelings before disappearance of Maya etc .By the time we were back home, the sky was bright and time was 6.30 AM. Also, I showed him the paper containing Chaaya's address which came to me flying, when we reached home. Swaroop was in total confusion and after a cup of coffee he threw himself on the bed. Also, there was no discussion on the matter further, during his stay.

It was the D-Day of departure of Swaroop back to US. His route to Atlanta was via Paris. The Air France flight was in the early morning to Paris .The taxi arrived at midnight and three of us were in Airport by 1.30 AM. All the three were outside Departure lounge as there was sufficient time for Swaroop to proceed due to his telecheck- in.

We were highly emotional and were keeping mum. Swaroop broke the silence "Papa, why don't you write the story of your Maya like Harry Potter of J.K Rowling? Your Maya may out shine Harry Potter". This was sounding like joke but was his suppression of emotions in reality.

"Papa, Jokes apart, pl take care. Don't go for adventures .You better change your route and timing of walk" was the fraternal advice from son.

With a big hug to both and uncontrollable tears, Swaroop entered the departure lounge.His parting wave made us to feel as orphans. It was a difficult task for me to console Sudha. When w e were back home it was 4.30 AM. For the next few days I avoided my morning walk as I never felt like going.

The barking noise made me to wake up and the time was 4.30. With desistance I got up and got ready in my usual way for the morning walk. Sudha was fast asleep. In total dilemma of whether to follow my regular route or to take a different route, I stepped out of the house. Suddenly, I became spirited with high energy level and started moving briskly. After a few minutes I realized that I was in my original track of morning walk. Simultaneously, came to my mind the Maya's words ". I will be in you as a driving spirit boosting your energy and morale ".as a flash. My spirited walk continued with the feeling of Maya leading me. I was feeling bad for having forgotten Maya's promise.

"The only thing that can hallow Marriage is Love

and

the only genuine marriage is that which is hallowed by Love"

Leo Tolstoy

DIALOGUE WITH THE DEATH GOD

Dialogue With The Death God

Hosur, I don't know whether to call it a town or a village. If you look into the geographic area it is big enough to be called as town. But if we go by the population, life style of people, environment, wide spread cultivated lands and the landscape it is more a village than a town. Anyway, let us call Hosur as a big village.

Shankarappa, one of the residents of Hosur, even though not very rich, a fairly well to do person with about 30 acres of land and spacious house in the midst of garden. He basically not an educated and villager at core and has a well planed family with only one son. Also, he is one of the respected few in the village. Ramesh is his only son who is naturally the pet of the parents. The specialty of him is, in spite of being only son and also brought up with lots of love and care is not a spoilt brat, but a disciplined one. Another thing about Ramesh being, he is a bit different from other children of his age not playful, not mingling with many friends. The other peculiarity being, even at his early age of boyhood he developed the habit of strolling alone in the outskirts of Hosur enjoying the looks of green cultivated lands, sleeping under the shades of tree and plucking tamarind from the trees etc. In a way he is more an aloof conscience and an introvert.

Now, Ramesh is in his teens and studying in 10th standard in the high school of Hosur. The habit of solitary strolling has become part of his life. As a grown up boy he likes walking for long distances enjoying lush green fields and silence of the countryside. These days he is experiencing unusual incidents of sighting a strange looking person now and then in the outskirts during his walk. Also, surprisingly he gets the death message of somebody or the other invariably, whenever he sees that alien. Even though he gets doubt about the connection between the appearance of the strange man and the occurrence of death at Hosur, he never took it seriously thinking as a mere coincidence.

On that day, somehow, Ramesh felt like going out for a walk right in the morning and left home at around 6.15AM. It was a beautiful morning of late winter with the combination of mist and the early Sun rays. He was old enough to enjoy the nature and so was he with his mind fully open for various thoughts. However, his thoughts were more about his fast approaching exams than anything else. He was in the midst of lavish green paddy fields and it was absolutely silent al round except the chirping sound of the birds. Suddenly, he stopped with a shock as that strange man was sighted at a little distance in front of him. The look of him was so fearful that Ramesh ran away from there and reached home totally confused. This was so, as during his earlier meetings he had seen the Alien from a distance and hence was not able to get the real picture of him. On that day being Sunday there was no school and he confined himself to his room thinking only about that incident. The sound of crying in the living room woke him up from his nap suddenly at about 2PM.He came out of his room in anxiety and heard the news of sad demise of his uncle. Spontaneously tears rolled out from his eyes and also the incident of the morning appeared on his mind causing mental trauma.

In South India generally 14th January is celebrated in a big way as "Makara Sankranti" festival especially by the farmers. The significance of that day being, both men and cattle together in processions with lots of fun and frolics bringing a festive mood to the whole village. It was a Sankranti day and Shankarappa's house was buzz with activities with visiting friends and relatives right from morning. Ramesh was fed up with the disturbing noise and movement of the visitors in the house. Also the festival lunch had made him to feel heavy. Though the dusk was setting in, the evening was quite bright. Ramesh, to get away from the madding crowd went out for a walk. He was feeling better in the outskirts of the village and was also enjoying the look of Sunset. Unfortunately that pleasure was short lived with sudden appearance of that Strange looking man. He was flabbergasted with that shocking surprise. "Ramesh, Ramesh, what happened to you, why are you sweating so much" the anxious words of his mother made him to realize that he was back home. He was totally unaware of how he came home and what happened after he met that strange man. He was sitting in one corner of his room totally dazed.. Sudden hush in the festive activities made Ramesh to come out of his room suspecting some problem. His suspicision was true. The death news of Rangamma a distant relation and the neighbor was being talked by the people gathered there. He was convinced that the appearance of the strange man and occurrence of death in the village has definite relationship and is not just coincidence. He lost his mental stability and went to the state of depression.

Shankarappa and his wife were very much worried with change in behavior of Ramesh as they were not able to understand the reason behind this. Any amount of counseling and probing did not help in getting the facts behind this change. They consulted the local doctor also. Finally, they sent him to Blore to his uncle's place expecting improvement due to change of environment in spite his classes being on. With all their efforts quite a lot of   improvement was found after his return. To avoid recurrence, he was never allowed to be alone. So also his walking in the outskirts of Hosur was totally stopped. His increased interest in studies and the seriousness for the preparation for the fast approaching final exam. made him to come out of that trauma much earlier than the expected. By second week of April he completed his final examination and was very happy because of his good performance. He decided to visit Blore again and spend his holidays with his uncle.

After having real good time for about three weeks he was back in Hosur. For a few days, he was feeling bored after experiencing busy life of Blore and also there was nothing much at Hosur to spend time meaningfully. His parents were very watchful about his movements not allowing him to go here and there due the earlier bitter experience. We human beings may take holiday whenever we want. But "Time takes no Holiday". The time had gone on and Ramesh returned to the normal life of Hosur.

Ramesh had belly full of lunch and was feeling heavy and Dad and Mom were in their afternoon sleep. It was a cloudy afternoon perfect to take walk especially for youngsters, which lured him to go out. His mind was full of thoughts about his future after 10th std. After walking about two Kms, he was attracted by the beautiful shade of the Neem tree and felt like taking a nap, as he was feeling drowsy. The soothing breeze and the tenanting shade made him to have a sound sleep. He got up suddenly after an hour and started walking in a hurry to reach home fast thinking his mom would be worrying about his absence from the house. To his misfortune, the specter figure was coming towards him at a distance. Ramesh, who had forgotten this figure almost, was aghast because of the unexpected appearance. Not able to withstand the shock, he slid under the tree by the side of the road without understanding what was happening to him with the eyes closed. When he recovered after sometime there was no trace of the alien and he started running to reach home fast. He must have gone for about half a Km or so, that figure was seen again moving in front of him. Suddenly, Ramesh became spirited and was a different man with all the fear vanquished. Now he started following the stranger calling him "Sir, Sir". But, there was no response; he didn't turn back even. Ramesh didn't give up chasing and continued calling him again and again. After sometime the Alien stopped and looked back. He was very different from human beings to look at with distinct physique and very bright eyes. Ramesh was undeterred and with full of spirit asked the stranger "Sir, who are you? What is the relationship between your appearance and the occurrence of death in our village?". With a smile he said 'Death" and proceeded further. Ramesh could not understand immediately but realized after a while that the alien was no other than God of death. In contrast to getting scared Ramesh was emboldened and was running behind relentlessly shouting and screaming at the stranger "sir, can you tell me when I will die". There was no response and he was walking silently. Ramesh was determined and his chase was continuing. After about fifteen minutes the stranger came to a halt. This time there was no smile on his face but with a grunted voice he replied "I cannot answer your question. But one thing I promise. Before I come to take you there will be four clues and they will manifest as certain changes in your body. I may come at any time after the fourth clue." Immediately, the alien vanished leaving Ramesh in a totally traumatic condition. He was so much perturbed that he was unable to discern whether that occurrence was a reality or a wild dream. With great difficulty he reached home. By that time the strange man had played his trick. The death news of Siddanna a local leader and a close associate of his family, was waiting adding ineffable misery.

"Time flies". Days, months and years rolled out in Ramesh's life and many events took place. Some turned experiences.

"Events only become experiences through the interest we take in them. If they do not interest us, we are making nothing of them."

He completed his schooling and Pre University at Hosur and did his graduation at Bangalore. Shankarappa, his Dad was very much against his taking up job, as he wanted his son to look after his lands and stay with him at Hosur. But, Ramesh was very particular about taking up job and with great resistance he joined State govt. services. After sometime he married Arundhati. As he was in state govt. job he had regular transfers and due to this he was compelled to be away from Hosur most of the time. However, he had made many trips in the pretext of attending functions or festivals during this period. Also during his stay, he used to go out for walks in the outskirts as he used to do earlier with no trace of that specter figure anymore.

"Let the dead past bury its dead"

In everyone's life some of the dead past come alive as reminiscences now and then making either to repent or rejoice. Even though many of the past events of life had faded, Ramesh's experience with the strange man and his four clues remained afresh in the corner of his mind. Whenever this thought arose, he used to look for Alien's clues on his body and get emancipated after not finding them, thinking his death is still far off.

"Ignorance is bliss"

Finally, Ramesh retired from service after working for about 35years.Though he had enjoyed and liked the life of towns and city, he decided to spend his remains of life in his native. Arundhati, his wife was not very happy with his decision of settling down at Hosur, was forced to accept looking into the various positive aspects of his husband's decision. By the time they came to Hosur, both Shankarappa and his wife were no more. Ramesh and Arundhati got used to Hosur's life quickly. They were comfortable in all respects except that they were not having children which was the nagging pain swerving them always.

On that day, right from morning Ramesh was very uncomfortable with no interest of any sort. Around 2PM he started his lunch, as he was not able to relish he got up in between and walked straight to his bed room .His state of mind was such that he was not able to hear the call of his wife "Why, what happened to you .Are you not feeling well? He just lied down on the bed. After sometime he got up suddenly with a shock as if he had some wild dream. Unable to bear the torment, he shouted "Aundhi, get me a cup of water immediately". His shouting made her to come out running from kitchen with glass of water. He drank the water and as it was unbearable to sit inside the room he came out slowly taking the help of his wife. There was mild breeze of the evening outside soothing and he sat in the verandah stretching his legs on the floor. Although he was feeling better externally his mental agony was in increase every moment. He just closed his eyes and went for a nap.

"Ramesh, Ramesh, Get up, it is getting late, come on, let us go" the whispering words made him to open his eyes. O! Gosh! His eyes couldn't just believe .The Alien was in front of him. Now the person before him was not looking just strange but fearsome with bright eyes staring at him without a blink. Ramesh was totally aghast and dumbfounded. The specter figure once again said "Ramesh, come on, now is the time for me to take you". It took sometime for him to realize that the person standing in front was no other than his own death. Inexplicably, a strange thing happened and an unusual energy developed in his body, which gave him an oblivious courage.

He started asking the Alien "O! God of death, you are also known as 'Yama Dharma' God of justice, how you could do such an injustice to me. You broke your promise and have come to take me without giving even one of the four clues you had promised".

The death God smiled at him .The smile was sarcastic as if he was mocking at the manifestation of ignorance by Ramesh. He said "Ramesh, before accusing me go back to your yester years and recollect the past happenings of your life. Perhaps, you may not be able to do that now. Let me make you to remember." Immediately, Ramesh felt as if the lightening has struck and bright light entered into his mind. He felt enlightened. The God of death started narrating.

"Ramesh, you had come to Mysore on transfer from Tumkur and you were 30years old. You had good neighbors and were enjoying the company of those people. One day a smart girl in her teens who was the daughter of one of them came to your house as she used to do often. She said "Uncle, how is that you have so much of gray hairs? I think you have become old." with a naughty laugh. She further told, "Uncle, why are you not using Hair dye?" These words made you to feel bad. After a few days, you were standing in front of the mirror and praising yourself as you had beautiful shining black hairs. The change brought in you due to hair dye made you to forget that the graying of hair was the first clue given by me.

One day you told your wife "Arundhi, I am not able to see the letters properly and finding it difficult to read now a days. For that your wife said you are already Chaalis (meaning forty) and is the time for you to wear chhalish (meaning spects). Both of you enjoyed the joke by teasing each other. The day you went to your office with a stylish spectacle bought in one of the most popular shops of Mysore, all your colleagues and friends complimented saying, "you look like a real cine hero and spects suits you very well". With those praising words you felt yourself a real hero. In this excitement of looking young and smart with regained sight, you failed to identify my second clue. That is, loosing the normal eye sight requiring spects to regain.

You were already 53 and had already lost a few teeth. The remaining some were shaking and giving terrible pain. Sometimes you felt like getting rid of them all. You went to the best dentist of

Bangalore for advice. After started wearing dentures you felt relieved and also there was improvement in your look. In this process you again failed to recognize the third one, the characteristic change in your body; loosing the teeth.

It was seven years of living at Hosur after your retirement. Fortunately, you didn't have any other health problem except that you used to get joint pain and back pain now and then. This kept increasing and finally you were finding it difficult to walk. There was no other go and became a three legged man with a walking stick in your hand. With the third leg and some of the medicines you were almost back to your original activities. This illusion made you to forget my fourth and the final clue.

It is pitiable that you being educated and fairly knowledgeable, were not prepared to accept the cognizance of changes taking place in your body, as my clues. You were in different world thinking only about the lure of life and were totally nonchalant about the other face of life "the death". Also ignored the fact that "Death does not blow trumpet". As the Death God finally said "Jaathasya Maranam Dhruvam (meaning Death is definite when once born)"a gleam came out and Ramesh who was leaning to the verandah wall just slid on to the floor. Also there was no trace of the Alien.

Ramesh died at the age of seventy and he was buried in one of his lands as per his wish. His tomb still exists in Hosur as if it is mocking at the livings "Men may come and men may go, but I shall remain" The news of deaths are being heard often at Hosur, but the incidents of appearance of Strange man is never heard.

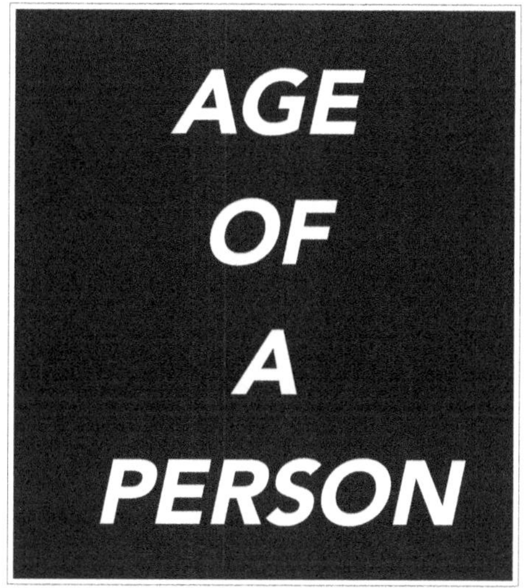
AGE
OF
A
PERSON

Preface

In the modern day living of false values and confused thinking, we are so much involved in looking for quicker solutions rather than nearer to nestle solutions for our problems. Even though most of us know the Spirituality/Spiritual path is the only way for long-term solutions, our analytical minds look skywards for deliverance.

The holistic life or living well for better quality of life can be achieved only through the entry to the spiritual realm.

Age of a Person

When somebody asks our age, we immediately look back to our date of birth and after doing some arithmetic we will tell our age as so and so. Recently, I happened to attend a discourse and in that an interesting story was narrated which goes like this:

There was a small town and in that lived a Sanyasi (Saint) who was quite young. His livelihood was the alms he used to get from the begging in that town. One day when he was on his routine, he visited a house and prayed for alms. A young and charming lady came out of the house and offered him the alms. The Sanyasi after seeing that beautiful lady got disturbed and felt like spending sometime with her. So, he decided to enter into conversation with her. As he didn't find topic to start immediately, he asked her age. Respecting the Sanyasi she replied spontaneously as "One year". Surprised with her answer he repeated the question seriously. Once again the reply was same "one year". He was annoyed thinking that lady to be arrogant, he asked the age of her husband. The reply was much more surprising and she said six months. This time Sanyasi felt as a great insult and said "you young lady, just because I have come for alms you can not insult me like this with your indifferent answers and make fun of me. Are you sure your age is one year and your husband's six months?" The lady was very cool and calm and with due respect to Sanyasi she said, "Yes sir". He was perplexed with her answer and kept mum for sometime. Then he asked the age of her In-Laws. The answer was "Three months". With her reply, Sanyasi started thinking seriously and felt there must be some secret in her replies He cooled down completely and asked "Miss, could you explain to me the basis of your quoting the ages as one year, six months and three months". Immediately the lady went inside the house, brought a seat and made the Sanyasi to sit comfortably in the verandah. She offered cool drink and explained

"Sir, I am physically 21 years old. But, just a year back I started thinking about the life, purpose of Life, Life after death etc. and realized that understanding of these things apart from needs of food, shelter and clothing are very essential to lead satisfied life. In other words, the Spiritual awareness has set in and Spiritual growth is taking place in me in this one year. I feel only this one year is worth in my age of 21 and mentioned my age as one year.

Coming to the age of my Husband, I advised him a year back when I started realizing the importance of these aspects. He never bothered at that time. I don't know what happened! Since six months he has inclined towards spirituality and I am finding some spiritual growth in him. I am really happy about this change, that's how I mentioned his age as Six months.

Regarding my In-Laws, even at the age of almost seventy, they were never interested in these matters and were thinking only about their money, assets children and other materialistic things. Thank God, at last some sort of realization of importance of spiritual matters is getting in them in the past three months. I hope this would continue and lead them to a worth life before they die. This recent three months of them I felt as their real age. I think, now you agree with me Swamiji."

After hearing her, the Sanyasi got up suddenly from the seat, left all the alms he had collected and walked out. The lady was surprised, called him and asked the reason for doing that.

"Even though, I am 24years old and calling myself Sanyasi, I never bothered about Spiritual aspects of life till today. Instead, I cheated others and myself in the disguise of Sanyasi to make my life easy and comfortable. I have committed great sin. I am so much grateful to you, as you made me to realize my mistake and showed the path of wisdom. As of today I have not even born on this earth with my 24 years of physical age a waste. How can I be eligible to accept alms" said the Sanyasi with wetted eyes and went away empty handed.

"To "live long" is almost everybody's wish, but to "live well" is the ambition of a few"

What does it mean, "Living well" - Is it the living with all the material comforts and luxuries in the world with the mind, heart and soul astray **or** Holistic life, a life style with physical, intellectual and spiritual well being. If the later is the answer, then Spirituality is only the one that can offer Holistic life in turn living well. Generally, when we talk of spirituality or spiritual path, we jump to look to a Sanyasi (Saint) who has relinquished the materialistic world and turned to penance. If the thinking is so, it would be a mistaken identity. As philosophers say "Spirituality is not separate entity. It is an integral part of our living. It bathes our passion with intensity and drive, as contentment is sought through the discovery of soul and surrendering to spontaneity." Aiso, the "Bhagavat Gita" the main theme of it no doubt is spiritualism, teaches in integrating spirituality in everyday activity of life. Therefore, when and how we adopt this, as a part of our living is one's choice.

In the modern day living of false values and confused thinking, we are so much involved in looking for quicker solutions rather than nearer to nestle solutions for our problems. Even though most of us know the Spirituality/Spiritual path is the only way for long-term solutions, our analytical minds look skywards for deliverance.

If we agree that a Holistic life is Living well for better quality of life, then, we have to look into two basic aspects..

1. To make contemporary living comfortable to the extent possible.

2. To understand the purpose of life that is "Who we are and what we are here to do"

Life, as all of us are experiencing, pitches us to a struggle phase with multifarious problems like illness, separation, relationship crisis, and financial problems so on so forth. This would result into STRESS due to flurry of brain activity and release of stress hormones. No doubt, stress to certain extent helps us to think, cope and work better, but beyond that point it starts tearing us apart. It is exactly at this zone, Spirituality works. It is said that "all, healing miracles and Godliness lie within us and all that spirituality does is to tap this sacred space to connect to the path relevant to contemporary needs. In other words, spirituality brings internal awareness helping to know how to back off and when. With a powerful relaxation response, we go into reverie and then to the agitating brain. It rids itself of the stress hormones and turns on feel good neurotransmitters like endorphins that smoothen the troubled waters of the struggle phase. Thus, imbalance and constrictions (called as Stress) at all levels reduce gradually and effectively making us comfortable.

The real power comes to us from knowing the "Goal of Life" that is "who we are and what we are here to do". To know this one must be able to find one's road map. This road map would be visible only if we dispel the darkness called Ignorance by throwing the light, the light of Wisdom. To find this light one has to enter into "Spiritual realm" which is within us as mentioned earlier. The personal road map or the path of wisdom once found, would lead us to grow beyond aggradations of base desires and narrow constricted selfish outlook and enlarge our vision. We also start offering something back to the society in turn to the world we are in. The offer, however small it is, helps us to move towards greater happiness and self-satisfaction.

To lead the holistic life which encompasses the above aspects, practicing Yoga is the emerging ray of hope. As modern day masters of "Power how" say, yoga is neither merely a mystical phenomenon nor an exercise in physical acrobatics. Yoga is simply a conscious and systematic process for the complete physical, mental, intellectual, emotional and spiritual development of human beings. In short, a methodical approach to "Self perfection" which in turn the guidance for Holistic life. Also, Bhagavat Gita says "Performance of one's duty rendered selflessly with dedication" is a spiritual path like Bhakti Yoga, Gyan Yoga, Karma Yoga etc. Which can lead a seeker to the Promised Land-the "Moksha"?

Epilogue

1. The compendium of the story of "Charming lady and Saint" we started with could be "When once born on this Earth, aging is natural and death is destined. During this aging, how far was holistic that only matters and would be the measure of one's "Real age" which is the resultant of one's spiritual growth.

2. The Yoga as I have read, is the knowledge of Body, Soul and God. This thought of Yoga lead me to write the following poem.

Song of the Soul

1. Oh, Death ! Am not afraid of thee,
   For, me(the Soul) an immortal,
   But, am feared of my remains(the Body) a mortal.
2. Oh, Death! Am not afraid of thee,
   For, me an insentient
   But, am feared of the miseries of remains, a Sentient.
3. Oh, Death! Am not afraid of thee,
   But, am feared of the agony you bring in to the remains,
   While me depart.
4. Oh, Death! Am not afraid of thee,
   For, me the imperishable.
   But, my remains do afraid of thee,
   For, thee a peril with me away.
5. Oh, God of Death! Don't be proud of thee
   For, you can perish my remains alone
   and not me,
   Me the Soul is the truth, supreme and Omniscient

www.ingramcontent.com/pod-product-compliance
Lightning Source LLC
Chambersburg PA
CBHW020121310726
48970CB00002B/735